MAX AND ELIZABETHAN ADVENTURE

BY SAMANTHA METCALF

ILLUSTRATED BY IAN R. WARD

Second edition
Published in Great Britain in 2020 by:
Mysteries in Time Limited
info@mysteriesintime.co.uk

Illustrated by Ian R. Ward.
www.ianrward.co.uk

A catalogue record for this book is available from the British Library.

ISBN 978-0-9935660-1-1

Hi! I'm Katie and I am 8 years old. Max is my older brother. He's really clever. He helps me with my homework when I'm stuck. He knows everything! But don't tell him I said that. He can get really annoying and know-it-all. He is always telling me stuff, but sometimes it's just too much. All I want is a simple answer, like 'yes' or 'no'. Instead, it's always 'maybe, because...' So annoying.

But he's not so bad. He always looks out for me. And we have fun playing games together.

I think my favourite thing is playing outside in any weather! I love going to the park, especially the adventure playground with the huge, curly slide. You can go really fast on that one, especially when you lie down! Mum hates it when I come home covered in mud, but I can't help it. The fun parts of the park are always the muddiest.

Hey, I'm Max and I'm 11. I love reading. I read comics and cartoons that make me laugh, and I read adventure stories about knights and castles, or pirates and buried treasure! Mum is always telling me I have an over-active imagination. I can't help it. My mind just starts picturing loads of weird stuff.

I also love solving puzzles. Grandpa always buys me books full of word-searches and crosswords. I like to time myself and see how fast I can solve them.

Katie is my younger sister. She is really energetic and fun to be around. She's really fast and sporty. I wish I could be as good as her at sports. But don't tell her I said that. She can also be really annoying, when she can't sit still for more than five minutes. And she doesn't stop talking!

But she's cool. I'm pleased she's my sister.

1

It was Saturday morning and Max and Katie were bored. It was nearly a month since their last adventure had ended and they had nothing to do. Well, they had loads of things they *could* do, like tidy their bedrooms, help Mum unpack the shopping, wash the breakfast dishes... but nothing they *wanted* to do. They were still in their pyjamas watching cartoons on the TV, when they heard a knock on the front door. They looked at each other. Could it be..? Surely not...

They listened carefully. They heard the front door open, then muffled voices. The door closed. Mum's footsteps came towards the lounge. Max and Katie were now on the edge of their seats, waiting.

Just when they couldn't bear it any longer, their mum opened the door with a big smile on her face.

"Ta-dah!" she sang happily. "There's..." Max was

already on his feet. He had taken the parcel from his mum's out-stretched arms and was already halfway up the stairs before his mum could even finish her sentence, "... another parcel for you."

Upstairs, Max and Katie eagerly opened the box.

"Where will we go this time?" asked Katie impatiently.

Max started to read the Mission Plan.

Mission Plan

Place: London, England
Date: 1593

In Elizabethan England, brave explorers sailed to new lands far away. They returned with new fruits and exotic spices, but also incredible treasure stolen from Spanish ships.

Spanish galleons were returning from the Americas with a great amount of treasure. The popular Queen Elizabeth I allowed her explorers to attack these Spanish ships, as long as she was given half of all the treasure they stole.

One day, the Queen was told that the most beautiful piece of treasure stolen from the Spanish ships (a large necklace covered in precious jewels) was missing. One of the sailors must have stolen it. Stealing from the Queen was treason. While hunting the thief in 1593, two innocent people were tortured and killed by the Queen's soldiers, but they never found the necklace.

Your Mission:

1. Find some Elizabethan clothes.

2. Travel back to London in 1593.

3. Find out what really happened to the necklace to save the lives of the two innocent people.

Good luck.

2

"Two innocent people were tortured and killed? This sounds like a dangerous adventure," said Max.

Max and Katie read the history fact book to learn as much as they could about Elizabethan times. Katie looked at Max with worried eyes.

"Do you think we'll be OK?" she asked. "I don't want to be stretched on the rack or burnt at the stake or get the bubonic plague or fall over in an open sewer or… or… or anything else horrible!"

"Don't worry," replied Max, trying his best to sound like a knowledgeable big brother. "We'll be fine. I will look after you."

"But who will look after you?" asked Katie.

That was a good question.

Max decided to distract themselves from their worries by finding some Elizabethan clothes.

"Let's go visit Grandpa."

3

Inside their grandfather's fancy dress shop, they looked along the rows of colourful, extravagant clothes that were labelled 'Elizabethan'. They had told their grandfather that they needed clothes for a school project, because the school was learning about Elizabeth I and the Spanish Armada this term.

Katie found a beautiful silk and velvet dress decorated with jewels, with pretty patterns stitched in silver thread. She held it up and pictured herself with a ruff around her neck and pearls in her hair.

When Grandpa wasn't listening, Max reminded her that they needed to blend in with normal people in the street to find out what had happened to the sailor's treasure. That meant they needed the clothes of poor people. Katie wasn't impressed.

"You just don't want to wear tights," she said.

Max didn't tell her she was absolutely right.

4

Back home, they got dressed. Katie had a white long-sleeved top with a long, blue skirt. She wore a white linen bonnet over her hair. She had a brown waist-coat, laced at the front, and a white apron over her skirt. Max wore long, woollen socks with dark green puffy shorts, a loose, white tunic and a brown, sleeveless jacket. He also pulled on a brown cap.

After admiring their reflections in the mirror, Max held out the Time Travel Sticker to Katie.

"I thought the point of the Time Travel Sticker was to translate any foreign language for us. Why do we need a translator this time?" asked Katie. "We are staying in England!"

"The Time Travel Sticker actually has two jobs. Yes, it acts as a translator, but its second job is to transport us back to the modern day after we have solved the mystery. It's a very clever little computer!"

explained Max. "Besides, they still talked differently back then." He cleared his throat and looked serious. "Good Morrow, mine sister. Prithee, come hither."

Katie just looked at him. "I think you've gone mad, you're speaking gibberish!"

Max explained that he was speaking English, but it was the English that people spoke in England 400 years ago. "I actually said: Hi Sis'. Come here, please."

Katie shrugged her shoulders and leant over to get her Time Travel Sticker. Her frown turned into a smile when she saw the sticker.

"It's a pretty flower!" she exclaimed happily.

"It's the Tudor Rose," explained Max. "It's the symbol of the kings and queens in the Tudor family. Queen Elizabeth I was a Tudor."

Katie didn't really care. She just knew that she liked it.

It was time to turn on the time machine. Max programmed it to take them to London in 1593. They prepared themselves for the whirlpool of time travel and pushed the button.

Max watched with excitement as the familiar mess of colour began to spin around them. He enjoyed this part of the magical ride. Soon, though, they both started to feel dizzy and shut their eyes firmly.

After a few minutes, they felt like they were slowing down and the world was returning to normal. They felt solid ground beneath their feet and opened their eyes. They looked around.

Something wasn't right.

5

It was almost dark. They were on a dirty, dusty street with a lot of people rushing around in every direction. Long skirts swirled around them. Dust was kicked up and there was a strong sense of fear in the air. Everybody was desperate to be somewhere else. Anywhere but here. But why?

Max and Katie clung to each other so they didn't get separated in the confusion.

Just as the crowd started to scatter, they heard a loud rumble. It was getting louder and louder. They turned around. They were standing at the bottom of a small hill and a huge wooden cart was hurtling towards them, about to run them over. It was out of control.

There was nowhere to go. People were everywhere. They heard the cart get closer– it was about to hit them!

Max and Katie opened their mouths to scream as they shut their eyes tight, expecting the worst. They threw their arms up to protect themselves.

6

Suddenly, they both felt as if they were flying
through the air.

"I'm a ghost! You're a ghost. We're both ghosts!"
wailed Katie. "I'll never get to taste ice-cream ever
again!"

Max thought there were more important worries
about being dead than never having ice-cream again.
He opened one eye, then two.

"You're both fine, don't worry," said a gentle
voice behind them. They both looked round. A lady
wearing a long brown dress was smiling at them. She
had a hand on the back of Max's top and another
hand on the back of Katie's dress. She had pulled
them both back at the last minute. She had saved
them!

Katie clapped her hands in delight, but before
they had time to thank their rescuer, the lady opened

the wooden door of the house beside her and ushered them inside.

"Quick, it's safer inside. That's the dead cart," she said, closing the door behind them. "You mustn't get close to that."

"The d-d-d-dead cart?" stammered Katie, nervously. "How can a cart be dead? It was never alive!"

The lady smiled. "It's how they collect the dead bodies, the poor victims of the terrible plague. You can still catch the sickness even after those poor people have found peace."

Max and Katie shivered. They were pleased they never saw the dead bodies. And even more pleased they weren't ghosts themselves.

7

They were now sitting on small stools at a wooden table in this lady's simple house. Katie looked around. On one side of the dark room there was a large grate with an open fire. A pot was balanced above the flames.

The lady introduced herself as Joan.

"I'm Max, this is my sister Katie," replied Max.

"Very pleased to meet you. You both had quite a scare out there," she said as she stood up and walked to the large pot that was bubbling away. "You should eat some pottage to get your strength up again."

Katie looked at Max, waiting for him to explain. He leaned over. "Pottage is like a stew or a thick soup with lots of vegetables," he whispered.

Katie rolled her eyes. She hated vegetables. They were so boring.

Max smiled. "You should be pleased. Thank

goodness it's not something weird like rabbit or pigeon!" he whispered back.

While Joan's back was turned, Max looked around. There were two shelves that stretched all along the wall opposite the front door. The shelves held glass jars of different shapes and sizes, all filled with unrecognisable herbs and spices. There were roots and tree bark, flowers and powders.

Max's eyes followed the colourful display along the wall, until he saw something strange. In the last few jars... no, it couldn't be... Max leaned closer. Was it really..? He saw slimy brown skin and webbed feet. Lots of webbed feet. All suspended in clear liquid. He read the label: 'Leg of Toad'.

Why on earth did Joan need 'Leg of Toad'? Max couldn't think of any reason why anyone would need toads' legs. Unless you were a toad.

Katie looked at her brother. "Max, are you OK? You have turned an odd shade of green."

The last thing he heard was his sister's voice. "Watch out Max!"

8

Max opened his eyes and realised he was lying down. "Wh-what happened?" he asked groggily.

"You fell off your chair," explained Katie. "I was worried. I thought maybe you'd caught the plague." Max realised he must have been leaning too far, trying to read the labels on the mysterious jars.

"Don't worry, Max," replied Joan. "It's not the plague. But you did cut your arm when you fell." Max looked down at the scrape on his arm. Joan was mixing a thick, green paste in a little wooden bowl.

Max remembered the strange things in the jars and wondered what she was making. "Er, wh-wh-what is in there?" he stammered, pointing with his free arm.

"This is a simple herbal ointment that should help your skin heal and keep infection out," she explained. She smiled and looked at him. "Don't worry, they're all natural ingredients that grow in my garden. Nothing from those jars at the end that you were trying to look at."

Max felt his cheeks get hot with embarrassment. He watched with interest as she applied it to his cut arm. "Wow, that feels so much better!"

Joan smiled. "I wish everyone reacted like that. Many people call me a witch because I use herbal ingredients. They call them potions, but it's all natural. I usually just use plants and herbs, nothing dangerous." She pointed up to the end jars. "They're special ingredients. I don't use them very often."

Joan served them some pottage with stale-looking bread. They wolfed it down. "This is really tasty!" exclaimed Katie, surprised.

Joan went to clean everything away, but got distracted by something through the window. She started to bite her fingernails with worry.

"Is everything OK, Joan?" asked Katie.

9

"Oh, it's just terrible. Terrible!" replied Joan.
"There is no hope for poor Edward across the road.
He is such a kind, gentle man. And helpful. He
always helps me carry the wood from the market."

"What's happened to him?" asked Max.

"He's fallen ill. It is probably the plague. I actually
hope it *is* the plague, for his sake," cried Joan.

Katie was shocked. "Why on earth would you
hope it's the plague? He's your friend!"

Max hoped she wouldn't hope the plague on
anyone at all, but he didn't say this out loud.

"Oh, it's quite complicated. You see, Edward
was once a sailor for Queen Elizabeth's navy. He's a
brave hero who fought the Spanish Armada!" Joan
wiped her nose noisily on her sleeve. "But many
years ago, he was on board Sir Francis Drake's ship,
the Golden Hinde, when they attacked the Spanish

galleon, the Cacafuego." She looked at Max and Katie, waiting for them to understand. They didn't.

"What happened?" asked Katie.

"Well, there was a treasure chest on that Spanish ship that Sir Francis Drake claimed for himself and his country. The best piece was a spectacular necklace made of the bluest sapphire, surrounded by sparkling diamonds, set in the purest gold you have ever seen."

Max imagined the scene.

"Of course half of all treasure goes to the Queen. Sir Francis Drake described this necklace in such detail to Queen Elizabeth, that it was the only piece she was interested in. But it went missing before it could be given to her. Disappeared into thin air. It had to be someone on board that ship who took it." Joan looked at Max and Katie. "I've heard rumours."

"Do *you* think Edward took it?" asked Max.

Joan's eyes sparkled as she smiled through the tears. "Yes. If it's really as impressive as they say, then I think he probably did take it. Now that he's an old man, too old to work, he probably tried to sell it."

Katie was confused. "But this doesn't explain why you would want your friend to die from the plague."

"I don't want him to die at all," she cried. "But those soldiers are here to arrest him. Stealing from the Queen is treason. If someone has told them that Edward is the thief, he'll be tortured and executed in the most painful way, probably on the rack." She shivered.

"Dying from the plague would be a blessing."

10

Katie walked to the window and looked out across the road. Sure enough, there were two soldiers standing guard outside Edward's front door. They wore silver armour on their chest and a curved helmet. They each carried a tall stick with a sharp blade on the end that looked like an enormous axe.

It was dark outside now, and the soldiers had lit a fire to keep themselves warm. They rubbed their hands together and jiggled from foot to foot. Their clouds of breath looked ghostly in the cold air.

Just as Katie was about to turn away, her eyes were drawn to the left, where a strange creature was approaching the soldiers. Katie opened her mouth but no sound came out. Max saw his sister freeze on the spot.

"What's wrong, Katie?" he asked.

Katie lifted a shaking arm and pointed across

the street. Max stepped to the window and followed her gaze. He understood her fear. There was a figure there with a very strange shape. It wore a long, thick robe with big boots and a wide-rimmed hat. Its fingers were as fat as sausages. But the strangest part was its face. Instead of a nose, it had a long, curved beak that cast scary shadows over the dirty street.

"Run!" whispered Katie. "Why don't those soldiers run?"

11

Max smiled, relieved. "Don't worry. It's not a monster," he explained. "That's just the doctor."

Katie's cheeks started to gain some colour back. "Doctor? Why is he in fancy dress?"

"The thick coat, gloves and boots stop the fleas from biting his skin and the mask stops him from breathing in any germs or infected air."

"But why does the mask have that silly beak?"

"It's filled with bergamot oil that smells like sweet perfume," explained Max.

Joan joined them at the window. "Don't worry," she said. "I gave the doctor a fresh amulet yesterday."

"An amulet is a lucky charm, isn't it?" asked Katie.

"Yes!" replied Joan. "The amulet I gave him is the pouch on his belt. It's full of crushed toads and dried blood. That will keep him safe."

Max remembered the toads' legs in the jar and

shuddered.

"Toads? DRIED BLOOD?" shrieked Katie.

Joan smiled. "Most of my potions only use herbal ingredients. But everyone knows that wearing dried blood and crushed toads keeps people safe from the plague." It was Katie's turn to shudder.

They watched the doctor approach the house. The soldiers stepped aside and let him enter. The door closed behind him.

"This is the moment of truth," she said softly, wiping away a tear. "We must wait and hope for Edward's sake that he does have the plague and it is a quick and painless death for him." She lit a tall, white candle in the window. Katie wrinkled her nose at the horrible smell that wafted from the candle.

Max whispered to her that poor people used candles made from animal fat. "That's why it smells."

"Urgh for the smell and double-urgh because it's animal fat," she whispered back, pinching her nose.

12

The candle was burning low. The doctor had been inside Edward's house for more than two hours now.

"What's taking him so long?" asked Joan. They had taken turns to watch Edward's house through the window. They had seen a lot of shadows in the upstairs window, lots of movement. "He's usually very quick to diagnose whether it's the plague or not."

"Maybe they're having a chat?" suggested Katie. "Or having a nice cup of tea. Or playing cards."

Max didn't have time to explain that tea was very new in Elizabethan England and not popular yet, because just at that moment Edward's door opened and the doctor emerged. The soldiers looked at the doctor, who shook his head, turned and hobbled away. Max noticed he walked with a limp and wondered how he had hurt his leg.

The soldiers looked sad as they hammered planks of wood across the front door and the windows,

"Why are they doing that?" shrieked Katie. "Nobody will be able to go in or come out!"

"Exactly," replied Joan gloomily, as she watched the soldiers paint a large warning cross above the door in red paint.

13

'The birds were waking up and soon it sounded like a chorus of tiny voices. The sun was starting to rise and the sky was painted with splashes of reds and pinks. A single cloud floated high above the city.

Everyone had dozed off, but something woke Katie. She heard hooves clip-clopping on the cobbled stones. A horse! Katie loved horses. She looked out of the window and saw a new soldier approach the house on horseback. He was riding a tall white horse that had strong, powerful legs.

This was clearly a soldier in charge. He looked cross. He shouted something at the two tired soldiers who had been on watch all night. He pointed at the boards on Edward's door angrily. The two soldiers looked at each other confused.

The soldier in charge shouted again. The two soldiers reluctantly turned and started pulling the boards off the door using their axe-shaped weapons.

"This makes no sense," said Joan after Katie had woken her and Max up. "The house should stay locked up for weeks to keep the sickness inside."

At that moment, the dead cart arrived. The soldiers held handkerchiefs to their faces, covering their mouths and noses as they stood back. The dead collectors raced inside and quickly emerged carrying something large, wrapped in a thick, dirty blanket.

Katie and Max looked away. They didn't want to see them throw Edward's body onto the pile of other plague victims. They heard the cart rattle away, leaving them with the gentle sound of the birdsong.

The soldiers looked again to the man on the horse, who pointed to the house before riding away. They took deep breaths of fresh air, covered their noses and mouths once more, then stepped inside.

"They must be searching for the necklace," said Joan. "I hope they find it so this matter can be over."

14

The sun was now shining bright in the sky, so Joan blew out the candle. The soldiers had been inside Edward's house for half an hour when a messenger arrived and summoned the soldiers out. They gulped fresh air as they read his note. Relieved, they boarded up the door again, then hurried away.

Joan, Max and Katie sat quietly for a while thinking about poor Edward.

After a short while, there was a frantic knock at the door and Joan opened it to find a lady who was out of breath. She came inside and sat at the table.

"Joan, it's terrible, really terrible!" she gasped, wringing her hands anxiously. "Christopher has been taken. They took him away. He's gone!"

Joan held up her two hands to slow her down. "Mary, calm down. What do you mean? Where has Christopher gone? Who took him?"

"The soldiers. They came a few minutes ago. They say he stole something that belongs to the Queen." The visitor suddenly burst into tears. Her shoulders shook. "But he's not a thief!"

Joan looked at Max and Katie. "Christopher is the local doctor," she explained. "Mary, before he was taken, did Christopher say why he was inside poor Edward's house for so long last night?"

Mary stopped sobbing and looked at Joan, puzzled. "Edward's house? Last night?" she laughed. "But that's impossible. He was over at Chancery Lane all night. Lady Anne gave birth to a little boy early this morning. He was there the whole night."

"But we saw the doctor here with our own eyes. How could he be in two places at once?" said Katie.

"Unless… unless that wasn't really the doctor last night," said Max. "We never saw his face. Does Christopher walk with a limp?"

Both ladies shook their heads.

"But why would someone pretend to be a doctor?" asked Katie. "And why would anyone want to enter a plagued house if they didn't need to?"

"The doctor's mask acted as a disguise, as well as keeping the thief safe from the plague," explained Max. "He must have been looking for the necklace that whole time last night. He knew nobody would interrupt him in a plagued house. Then all he had to do was hide it under his robes and walk out, right past the soldiers! They never even saw his face."

15

They all thought carefully about how to save Christopher. Together, they came up with a plan.

Joan and her friend would race to Chancery Lane and explain to Lady Anne what had happened.

"She's the only person who can prove that Christopher is innocent," explained Max. "Lady Anne must send a signed note to the soldiers in the Tower of London, proving that the real doctor was with her last night when the theft took place. It's the only way to prove that Christopher is innocent."

"But what if it takes too long?" cried Mary. "By the time we get a message from Lady Anne to the Tower, it may be too late for Christopher."

"We'll go straight to the Tower to tell the soldiers that they must wait for the message," said Max.

They must save him from torture.

Or worse.

16

Outside, Max and Katie had to pinch their noses.

"Urgh!" cried Katie. "What is that horrid smell?"

"There was no sewer system or rubbish collection in Elizabethan times," said Max. "You think this is bad? Imagine how smelly it got in the summer!"

They ran as fast as they could through the narrow London streets. The city was waking up. Women with long skirts were brushing dust from their doorsteps. Rats scurried along the open sewers. People emptied their chamber pots from upstairs windows. Max and Katie dodged all these obstacles and soon arrived at the Tower of London.

They were out of breath. "Doctor... innocent... Lady Anne... STOP!" gasped Max in short bursts.

They caught their breath and explained everything to the soldiers on the gate.

The guards listened, but looked at each other

unsure. The older man with a kind face nodded to his partner, who told Max and Katie to follow him. They crossed the moat by walking across the drawbridge then stepped into the dark corridors of the Tower's walls. They followed the guard through cool stone corridors and down winding stairs.

They came to a large door, which the guard pushed hard. They blinked as they stepped into sunlight on Tower Green. Max and Katie saw the White Tower in the centre of the grass, with its four stone towers at each corner. They walked towards it.

"It looks weirdly the same as it did on my school trip last year!" exclaimed Katie. Max shot her a warning look to keep quiet.

They entered a dark, damp room with a musty smell. This was clearly the dungeon; there were terrifying instruments of torture everywhere.

They approached a large wooden table in the centre. There was a wheel with a handle at each end.

Max recognised it immediately.

"The rack!" he gasped, horrified.

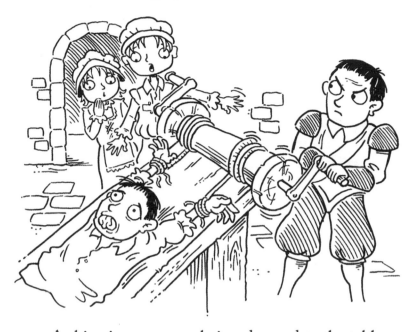

A shivering man was being dragged to the table. He was held down by two strong soldiers as two others tied his wrists and ankles to each corner of the table. He was trying to speak but there was a red rag pushed inside his mouth.

"Stop!" shouted Max to the soldier. He turned to the man on the rack. "Are you Christopher?"

The prisoner nodded at Max with surprised eyes.

"This man is innocent! You're making a terrible mistake! Let me explain before you hurt him."

The soldiers listened to Max's story. "I don't want to get in trouble with the Queen," said one soldier nervously. "But how do we know we can trust them?"

"Why don't we wait and see if this letter arrives?" suggested another guard. "He's not going anywhere."

"Good point. Let's lock the doctor back up and wait. We can always finish this later," a third replied. They all looked at Max and Katie. "Let's lock them up as well. If they are lying, we will start with them."

Max and Katie were dragged to a windowless cell and thrown inside with the doctor. They banged on the door as the soldiers locked it noisily.

"Let us out!" they shouted. "We're innocent!"

"Don't waste your breath, said the doctor. Max and Katie looked at him. He was sat on the cold, stone floor in the corner. "Silence is good. It means nobody is being tortured."

17

"Are you OK, Christopher?" asked Katie.

"A few bruises. But I'll be fine, all thanks to you," he smiled. "Where did you come from?"

"I'm Katie and this is Max. We are Joan's friends."

They explained what had happened, but it wasn't long before they heard footsteps outside. A large metal key was pushed into the lock and they heard it turn slowly. The door opened with a heavy creak and there stood the soldier from the gate outside.

"You're free to go," he said happily. "All three of you. You're very lucky, Doctor. If these two hadn't turned up, you would be a lot taller by now!"

The doctor shuffled out past the soldier.

"Besides, we have the real thief now," the soldier continued. "We realised that it must be witchcraft to make the doctor appear in two places at once. We have arrested the local witch. She lives opposite

Edward's house. She must have cast a spell to steal that necklace. We found lots of potions and strange objects in jars and bottles at her house."

Max and Katie stopped in their tracks. They turned around to face the soldier. "Joan? Where is she? What will happen to her?"

"She's a witch. She will be hanged at the gallows."

18

Max and Katie helped Christopher through the dark corridors to the Tower Green. They saw a huge wooden stage with a frame: the gallows. There was a young soldier humming a happy tune as he tied a thick rope to the top of the frame. Max's eyes were drawn to the end of the rope. To the noose.

Just then, they saw Joan being dragged past on her way to the dungeons. She looked terrified. Katie called out to her, but she was already gone.

"Come on, we need to hurry," said Max. They helped Christopher out through the Tower gates. Mary was there waiting and she threw her arms around Christopher's neck and sobbed with relief.

Max sat down on the grass to think. "The only way to save Joan is by finding the thief. Let's think about this," he said, feeling very frustrated. "Who would know that Edward had stolen that treasure?"

"Well, he was a sailor, and he stole it from the ship he was on. So…" thought Christopher out loud. "So maybe he had a partner in crime on the ship?"

Max looked up hopefully. "Yes! Another sailor! But how do we find him?" He looked out across the river to the ships in dock. "All we know is that he walked with a limp."

Mary had an idea. "The place you will most likely find a thief is down in Southwark, across the bridge."

"We also know that he can find a doctor's costume," added Katie.

Max shook his head at Katie and sighed. "They weren't costumes. They were protective clothes."

"Well they look very silly to me," shrugged Katie. "Like a fancy dress costume or a costume for a play."

She expected her brother to start giving her one of his lessons. She was surprised when he stood up, threw his hands on his head and laughed loudly. "Of course! You're right!'

19

Max told Christopher and Mary to stay close
to the Tower in case Joan got released. "Come on,
Katie, hurry up!" said Max as he set off at full sprint.

Katie was confused, but she caught up with Max
quickly. "Where are we going?" she called.

"We have to get to the other side of the river,"
replied Max over his shoulder. He didn't stop until
they reached a busy, crowded bridge.

"Ah, so this must be London Bridge!"

Katie looked puzzled. "London Bridge is much
prettier with two big towers and a drawbridge."

"You're thinking of Tower Bridge, and that wasn't
built until the 1800s," explained Max. "London
Bridge is just a normal bridge in modern day, but in
Elizabethan London it had houses built all along it."

Sure enough, people were starting to open their
doors and set up stalls in the street. Katie thought it

made more sense to live here than where Joan lived. At least here they got some breeze to blow away the horrible smells.

They continued forwards across the bridge. They passed chickens and goats. They saw beggars and pickpockets on the lookout for easy targets.

The buildings all along the bridge were tall. Some were at least six storeys high! In some parts, they had to walk through a dark tunnel underneath houses.

"It doesn't feel like we are on a bridge," said Katie. Max looked at the ceiling above and agreed.

They continued on. They were almost back on land when they stopped in their tracks. Katie screamed and covered her eyes. Max couldn't take his eyes off the gruesome sight in front of them.

At the entrance to the bridge there were tall sticks on each side. On the end of each stick there was a head. A dead person's head. The skin was grey and shrunken, but they were definitely heads.

20

Max grabbed Katie's hand and led her past the heads and off the bridge. They followed a road to the right, not stopping until the heads were out of sight.

"That was hideous," said Katie. "What was that?"

"They put the heads of traitors at the city gates as a warning to other people," explained Max. They walked a bit further, then Max stopped. "Look!"

Confused, Katie followed Max's pointed finger. They were standing outside the Rose Theatre. There were posters up announcing that Shakespeare's latest play, 'Henry VI', was closed. It was cancelled until the plague had passed.

"Do you see? You said it was a costume!" exclaimed Max. Katie shook her head in confusion. Max continued. "The theatre will have lots of costumes – maybe a doctor's costume!" he continued. "Katie, you really can be a genius sometimes!"

"What do you mean, 'sometimes'?"

Max and Katie waited only a short while before they saw a man with a limp approach. They were hidden behind a pile of boxes and crates, which were wrapped up in nets from the fishermen's boats.

Max and Katie watched him limp towards the theatre, looking around suspiciously. He was wearing a heavy coat that was tied tightly round the waist with a piece of rope. His hair was long and messy and he wore an eye-patch over his right eye. Max knew this was the same man they had seen outside Edward's house.

"Katie," whispered Max carefully. "You have to go and get help, find the soldiers and bring them here."

"What are you going to do? Surely we should stay together?" Katie was wide-eyed with worry.

Max knew he had to get inside the theatre.

"I'm going to follow him to see if I can find out where he put the necklace."

"But what if he sees you? He might be dangerous!" whispered Katie back.

"Don't worry," smiled Max. "He's got a limp and only one eye. I think even *I* can out-run him."

"OK, but be careful!" said Katie, getting ready to run back through London's narrow streets.

"You too," replied Max. "And run straight past the heads on the bridge! Don't look up!"

21

Max watched the thief limp to the theatre door, look around to check that he was alone, then enter. He was carrying something shiny in his hand.

Max waited until the door to the theatre was almost closed before he acted. He ran over and stuck his foot in the gap to stop it from closing. He waited a moment longer, listening, checking that the thief didn't come back. Nothing happened. He decided that it must be safe.

Max tiptoed over and gently opened the door. The coast was clear. It was like no other theatre Max had ever seen. It was round, with an open roof so you could see the clouds above. There were no seats on the ground level in front of the stage, only round the edge. There were three balconies on top of each other that curved round the edge with wooden benches where people could sit.

He heard a noise from the other side of the stage. It sounded like wood was being dragged across wood. He ducked back into the shadows and waited.

Soon, the thief stepped back from the edge of the stage, looked around, then left in a hurry. As the thief passed Max's hiding place, Max saw that his hands were now empty.

Max waited a short while to check that the coast was clear, then went to investigate what the thief had left behind. If it was the necklace, he could prove that Joan was innocent and save her life!

The other side of the stage looked undisturbed. There were steps leading up to the stage, but nothing unusual. Max was confused. He looked closer and saw that one of the floor boards below was loose.

Suddenly, he heard footsteps. Footsteps getting closer. Uneven footsteps. Someone with a limp.

The thief was coming back! He had less than a minute. He had no time to lose.

22

Max quickly pulled the board and it moved easily.

Inside, there was the most beautiful necklace he had ever seen. He knew he had no time to admire it now. He grabbed it and put it round his neck, tucking the pendant under his top. He slipped into the shadows beneath the stage, just in time.

Holding his breath, he waited. The thief appeared and saw the floor board had been moved and his secret space was empty. He stood up quickly, turned sharply and peered into the darkness.

"Who's there?" he croaked with a deep voice.

Max screwed his eyes shut and hoped that the angry thief would disappear and leave him in peace, as well as leaving him in one piece.

The room went very still. Silent. Max dared to open one eye a tiny bit, slowly. His eye came into focus and rested on a shape in front of him. He opened his other eye to make sense of what it was.

He realised he was looking at grubby fingernails attached to fat, hairy fingers, that emerged from a dark brown sleeve, which led his eyes to an angry face with lines on the forehead and a black patch covering one eye.

Max shouted in fright and ducked, just in time. The thief's hand grabbed thin air as Max dodged his attacker's grasp. He ran as fast as he could along the edge of the theatre. He could hear footsteps right behind him but he didn't dare to look around. He kept running. His heart was racing.

Max got to the front door and reached desperately for the handle. He had just closed his fingers around the metal handle, when he felt a hand on his shoulder. He yelled in terror and spun round to face his hunter.

23

"Max! It's me!" exclaimed Katie. "Relax! You're safe. I brought the soldiers."

Max blinked hard and gulped for air. "But... but... but he was right behind me!"

"We got here a minute ago. We heard you shout and we saw you running this way," Katie explained. "We waited until you had passed us and then the soldiers got ready to catch the thief."

Katie pointed to the middle of the theatre, where the soldiers were marching with the thief in between them.

"Phew, great timing, Sis!" Max high-fived his sister. "And look – I found the necklace."

Max pulled the pendant from under his top to show her. The sun was shining down through the open roof and the jewels dazzled brilliantly in the light.

"Woah, that is beautiful," exclaimed Katie. "So, er, nobody else actually knows that you, er, have this?"

"Sorry, Katie, we need to give this to Queen Elizabeth's guards to save Joan," replied Max.

"Shame," shrugged Katie. "But you're right. Let's go, before I change my mind."

24

Max and Katie returned to the Tower of London, where they once again met the same soldiers. They explained why they were there and they were led in through the Tower gates.

"I will take you to Sir Richard. He is the Queen's trusted friend. He will know what to do," explained the friendly guard.

They approached a gentleman, who was feeding bread crumbs to some ravens. The guard bowed deeply to him.

Max and Katie explained everything that had happened and showed him the necklace. He never took his eyes off the ravens while Max and Katie were speaking and only briefly glanced down at the necklace as he took it in his pale hand. He sighed heavily. "Ah, so we shall have no hanging today. Pity, I was looking forward to it."

Max and Katie looked at each other in horror. "Er, so, what will happen to our friend Joan?"

"Hmmm?" His distant daydream was interrupted. "Oh, yes. The witch. She will be freed. Shame."

They left the Tower as quickly as they could. They sat down by the river and waited. "Just being near that man made me shiver," said Katie. "He seemed like pure evil. I bet his head swivels right round."

Max didn't have time to agree, because Joan was released from the gates straight away. She spotted them waving and came over to hug them.

"How can I ever repay you?" she asked.

"Yes," agreed the doctor, who had just arrived. "Not only did you save our lives, but you saved us from the most painful death you can imagine." He shook their hands strongly. "Thank you."

Max smiled. "No problem! We're even! You saved our lives yesterday, Joan, remember? We are just pleased that we found the thief in time!"

"What will happen to him?" asked Katie.

"Well, they don't need to torture him, because they have found the necklace," said Joan. "He must also be a hero from the Spanish Armada. We can only hope that he won't be executed out of respect."

Christopher nodded. "But I imagine he will be punished somehow, maybe they'll hold him in the stocks for people to throw rotten vegetables at him."

Max and Katie happily waved goodbye to Joan, Mary and Christopher, then walked to a quiet garden next to the river where nobody could see them. They had time to take one last look around at Elizabethan England before the air started to spin and colours mixed together into a blue haze.

Safely back in his bedroom, Max shook his head. "I can't believe they used to kill people for being witches! I'm so pleased we live in the 21st century."

"Me too," smiled Katie. "Let's go get some ice-cream!"

The End.

See you on our next adventure.

Also in the Mysteries in Time series:

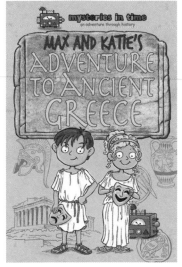

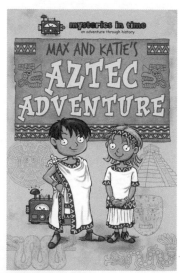

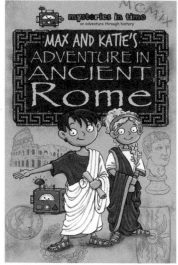